Nate
the
Great

Nate the Great

by Marjorie Weinman Sharmat
illustrated by Marc Simont

A Dell Yearling Book

Published by
Dell Yearling
an imprint of
Random House Children's Books
a division of Random House, Inc.
New York

Visit us on the Web! www.randomhouse.com/kids

Educators and librarians, for a variety of teaching tools, visit us at
www.randomhouse.com/teachers

ISBN: 0-440-46126-X
Reprinted by arrangement with Delacorte Press
Printed in the United States of America
One Previous Edition
December 2004
60
UPR

My name is Nate the Great.

I am a detective.

I work alone.

Let me tell you about my last case:

I had just eaten breakfast.

It was a good breakfast.

Pancakes, juice, pancakes, milk,
and pancakes.

I like pancakes.

The telephone rang.

I hoped it was a call to look for
lost diamonds or pearls
or a million dollars.

It was Annie.

Annie lives down the street.
I knew that Annie did not have
diamonds or pearls
or a million dollars
to lose.
"I lost a picture," she said.
"Can you help me find it?"
"Of course," I said.

"I have found lost balloons,
books, slippers, chickens.
Even a lost goldfish.
Now I, Nate the Great,
will find a lost picture."
"Oh, good," Annie said.

"When can you come over?"
"I will be over
in five minutes," I said.
"Stay right where you are.
Don't touch anything.
DON'T MOVE!"

"My foot itches," Annie said.

"Scratch it," I said.

I put on my detective suit.

I took my notebook and pencil.

I left a note for my mother.

I always leave a note

for my mother

when I am on a case.

Dear mother,
I will be back.
I am wearing my
rubbers.
Love,
Nate the Great

I went to Annie's house.
Annie has brown hair
and brown eyes.
And she smiles a lot.
I would like Annie
if I liked girls.

She was eating breakfast.

Pancakes.

"I like pancakes," I said.

It was a good breakfast.

"Tell me about your picture,"

I said.

"I painted a picture
of my dog, Fang," Annie said.
"I put it on my desk to dry.
Then it was gone.
It happened yesterday."

"You should have

called me yesterday,"

I said, "while the trail was hot.

I hate cool trails.

Now, where would a picture go?"

"I don't know," Annie said.

"That's why I called you.

Are you sure you're a detective?"

"Sure, I'm sure. I will find

the picture of Fang," I said.

"Tell me. Does this house have

any trapdoors

or secret passages?"

"No," Annie said.

"No trapdoors or secret passages?"

I said. "This will be

a very dull case."

"I have a door that squeaks,"
Annie said.

"Have it fixed," I said.

"Now show me your room."

We went to Annie's room.

It was big. It had yellow walls,

a yellow bed, a yellow chair,

and a yellow desk.

I, Nate the Great,

was sure of one thing.

Annie liked yellow.

I searched the room.

I looked on the desk.

And under the desk.

And in the desk.

No picture.

I looked on the bed.

And under the bed.

And in the bed.

The bed was comfortable.

I looked in the wastebasket.

I found a picture of a dog.

"Is this it?" I asked.

"No," Annie said.

"My picture of Fang is yellow."

"I should have known," I said.

"Now tell me. Who has seen

your picture?"

"My friend Rosamond has seen it,

and my brother Harry. And Fang.

But Fang doesn't count. He's a dog."

"Everybody and everything counts,"
I said. "I, Nate the Great, say
that everything counts.
Tell me about Fang.
Is he a big dog?"

"Very big," Annie said.

"Does he have big teeth?" I asked.

"Very big," Annie said.

"Does he bite people?"

"No," Annie said. "Will this
help the case?"

"No," I said. "But it might help me.
Show me Fang."

Annie took me out to the yard.
Fang was there.

He was big, all right.

And he had big teeth.

He showed them to me.

I showed him mine.

He sniffed me.

I sniffed him back.

And we were friends.

I watched Fang run.

I watched him eat.

I watched him bury a bone.

"Hmm," I said. "Watch Fang

bury that bone.

He buries very well.
He could bury other things.
Like a picture."
"Why would he bury
a picture?" Annie asked.
"Maybe he didn't like it,"
I said. "Maybe it wasn't
a good picture of him."
"I never thought of that,"
Annie said.
"I, Nate the Great,
think of everything.
Tell me. Does Fang ever
leave this yard?"
"Only on a leash," Annie said.
"I see," I said.

"Then the only place
he could bury the picture
is in the yard.
Come. We will dig in the yard."
Annie and I dug for two hours.
We found rocks, worms,
bones, and ants.
But no picture.

At last I stood up.

I, Nate the Great,

had something to say.

"I am hungry."

"Would you like

some more pancakes?" Annie asked.

I could tell that

Annie was a smart girl.

I hate to eat on the job.

But I must keep up my strength.

We sat in the kitchen.

Cold pancakes are almost as good

as hot pancakes.

"Now, on with the case," I said.

"Next we will talk

to your friend Rosamond."

Annie and I walked

to Rosamond's house.

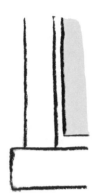

Rosamond had black hair
and green eyes.
And cat hair all over her.
"I am Nate the Great," I said.
"I am a detective."
"A detective?" said Rosamond.
"A real, live detective?"

"Touch me," I said.

"Prove you are

a detective," said Rosamond.

"Find something.

Find my lost cat."

"I am on a case," I said.

"I am on a big case."

"My lost cat is big,"

Rosamond said.

"His name is Super Hex.

I have four cats.

They are all named Hex."
I could tell that
Rosamond was a strange girl.
"Here are my other cats," she said.
"Big Hex, Little Hex,
and Plain Hex."
The cats had black hair
and green eyes.
And long claws.
Very long claws.
We went into Rosamond's house.
I looked around.

There were pictures everywhere.

Pictures of cats.

Sitting cats. Standing cats.

Cats in color

and in black and white.

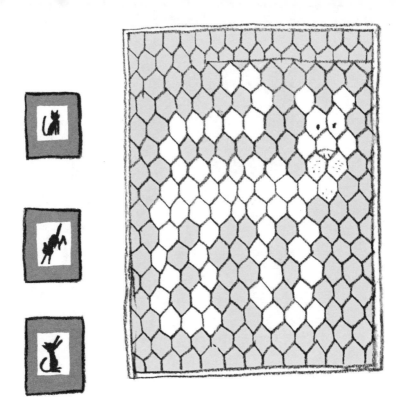

We sat down.

Little Hex jumped onto Annie's lap.

Plain Hex jumped
onto Rosamond's lap.

Big Hex jumped onto my lap.

I did not like Big Hex.

Big Hex did not like me.

"Time to go," I said.

"We just got here," Annie said.

She liked Little Hex.

"Time to go," I said again.

I stood up.

I tripped over something.

It was long and black.

It was a cat's tail.

"MEOW!"

"Super Hex!" Rosamond cried.

"You found him!

You are a detective."

"Of course," I said.

"He was under my chair.

Except for his tail."

Annie and I left.

It was a hard thing to do.

I could smell pancakes

in Rosamond's kitchen.

"Rosamond did not take
the picture of your dog," I said.
"Rosamond only likes cats.
And pancakes.
Now where is
your brother Harry?"

I met Annie's brother.

He was small.

He was covered with red paint.

"Me paint," he said.

"Me paint you."

"Good," I said. "No one has ever

painted a picture of me,
Nate the Great."
Harry took his paintbrush.
It was covered with red paint.
All at once I was covered
with red paint.

"He painted you," Annie said.

"He painted you."

Then she laughed.

I, Nate the Great, did not laugh.

I was on a case.

I had a job to do.

I looked around the room.

Harry had painted a clown,
a house, a tree, and a monster
with three heads.
He had also painted

part of the wall,

one slipper,

and a doorknob.

"He does very good work," I said.

"But where is my picture?"
Annie asked.

"That is a good question," I said.

"All I need is a good answer."

Where was the picture of Fang?

I could not find it.

Fang did not have it.

Rosamond did not have it.

Harry did not have it.

Or did he?

All at once I knew

I had found the lost picture.

I said, "I, Nate the Great,

have found your picture."

"You have?" Annie said. "Where?"

"Look!" I said. "Harry has a picture
of a clown, a house, a tree,
and a monster with three heads."
"So what?" Annie said.
"Look again," I said.

"The picture of the clown is red.
The picture of the house is red.
The picture of the tree is red.
But the picture of the monster
is orange."

"So what?" Annie said again.

"Orange is great for a monster."

"But Harry paints with red,"
I said.

"Everything is red but the monster.

I, Nate the Great,

will tell you why.

Harry painted a red monster

over the yellow picture of your dog.

The yellow paint was still wet.

It mixed with the red paint.

Yellow and red make orange.

That is why the monster is orange."

Annie opened her mouth.

She did not say a word.

Then she closed her mouth.

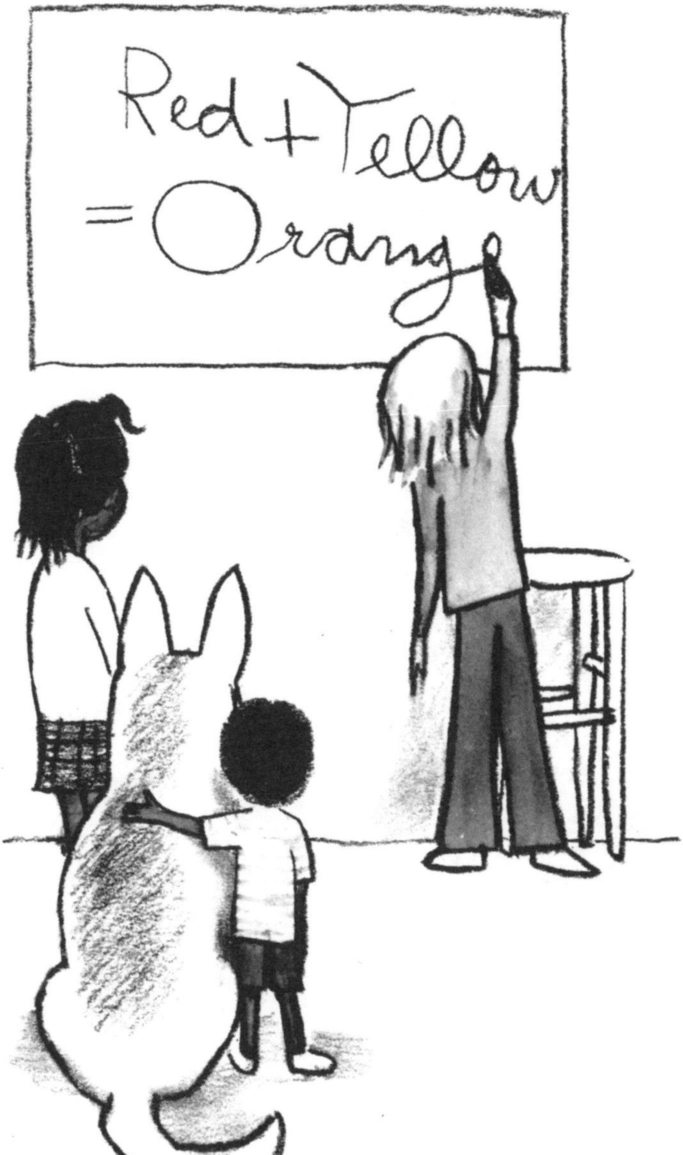
Red + Yellow
= Orange

I said, "See!

The monster has three heads.

Two of the heads were

your dog's ears.

The third head was the tail.

Yes, he *does* do good work."

Annie was very mad at her brother.

I was mad, too.

I, Nate the Great,

had never been red before.

"The case is solved," I said.

"I must go."

"I don't know how

to thank you," Annie said.

"I do," I said.

"Are there any pancakes left?"

I hate to eat on the job.

But the job was over.

We sat in Annie's kitchen.

Annie and I. And Harry.

Annie said, "I will paint

a new picture.

Will you come back to see it?"
"If Harry doesn't see it first,"
I said.
Annie smiled. Harry smiled.
They even smiled at each other.
I smiled, too.

I, Nate the Great,
like happy endings.
It was time to leave.
I said good-bye to Annie
and Harry and Fang.
I started to walk home.
Rain started to fall.
I was glad I was wearing
my rubbers.

~Extra~ Fun Activities!

What's Inside

NATE'S NOTES: Colors

Red, yellow, and blue are primary colors.
You can make all the colors in the rainbow
by mixing two of these three primary
colors together. But you can't make red,
yellow, or blue by mixing.

People are picky about colors. Most people
like blue toothbrushes. But when it comes
to cars, silver is tops.

Why do leaves change colors? During the summer, trees are busy turning sunlight, a gas called carbon dioxide, and water into sugar. Trees use the sugar as food. The trees make green pigment—or color—for their leaves because it helps the leaves soak up sunlight.

When winter comes, trees stop growing. They don't need food. So they stop making green pigment for their leaves. Without the green, the leaves' natural colors—reds and yellows—shine through.

Some animals change color, too. One is the chameleon. Most chameleons can change from green to brown and back to green. But a few can become almost any color.

Why would a chameleon want to change color? Nobody knows for sure. Here are some ideas:

Chameleons change color to match their surroundings. That may help them hide from animals that want to eat them.

They turn a darker color to keep warm. Dark colors absorb more heat than light ones.

Turning bright yellow or red might tell other chameleons "Look out! I'm in a bad mood!"

Boy chameleons might turn fancy colors to impress girl chameleons.

Rosamond's Crayon Cats Project

Rosamond likes to color. And she likes her cats. These cat crayons are purr-fect for her. You'll like them, too.

Ask an adult to help you with this project.

GET TOGETHER:

- broken crayons
- heavy paper cups
- an old spoon
- a pot holder
- cat-shaped candy molds*

* Look for these at craft stores. You can also buy them online.

MAKE YOUR CRAYON CATS:

1. Remove all paper from the crayons.
2. Sort the crayons by color. Or mix colors to see what happens.
3. Put the crayon pieces into the paper cups.
4. Place the paper cups in the microwave. Heat at half power for one minute. Stir. The crayons will still be lumpy. Heat and stir until all the lumps melt.
5. Using the pot holder, pour the melted crayons into the molds.
6. Place the molds in the freezer to cool.
7. Pop the cat crayons out of the molds. Use them to create something cool!

Nate's Pancake Recipe

Pancakes help Nate think. They're also good when you're hungry.

Ask an adult to help you with this recipe.

GET TOGETHER:

- a mixing bowl
- 1 cup flour
- a pinch of salt
- 2 tablespoons sugar
- $1^1/_2$ teaspoons baking powder
- 1 egg
- 2 tablespoons melted butter
- $1^1/_2$ cups milk
- a nonstick skillet
- syrup

1. In the bowl, mix together the flour, salt, sugar, and baking powder.
2. Add the egg, melted butter, and milk. Stir until just mixed together. Lumps are okay.
3. Warm the skillet over medium heat. Drop a tiny bit of water on the skillet. If the water skitters around, the skillet is hot enough.
4. For each pancake, pour about half a cup of batter onto the skillet. Wait until your pancakes have bubbles on top. Flip them. Cook them one more minute.
5. Put your pancakes on a plate. Pour syrup on top.
6. Eat (and think deep thoughts).

Serves one hungry detective, with leftovers for his dog.

Detective Talk

Detectives need to be tough. They like to sound tough, too. Here are some words to help you sound like a detective.

case: the mystery a detective is trying to solve.

client: the person who asks for a detective's help.

clue: a piece of information that helps the detective.

Some detective words are ordinary words with secret meanings.

Fishy usually means "smells like a fish." But when detectives say something is fishy, they mean it's suspicious.

A **stalk** is part of a plant. But detectives stalk— or follow—fishy-looking characters.

Pecan rolls are **sticky**—that is, gooey. But a sticky case is one that's difficult to figure out.

When detectives go **undercover,** it doesn't have anything to do with staying warm. It means they're working on a case in secret.

Have you helped solve all Nate the Great's mysteries?

❑ **Nate the Great**: Meet Nate, the great detective, and join him as he uses incredible sleuthing skills to solve his first big case.

❑ **Nate the Great Goes Undercover**: Who—or what—is raiding Oliver's trash every night? Nate bravely hides out in his friend's garbage can to catch the smelly crook.

❑ **Nate the Great and the Lost List**: Nate loves pancakes, but who ever heard of cats eating them? Is a strange recipe at the heart of this mystery?

❑ **Nate the Great and the Phony Clue**: Against ferocious cats, hostile adversaries, and a sly phony clue, Nate struggles to prove that he's still the world's greatest detective.

❑ **Nate the Great and the Sticky Case**: Nate is stuck with his stickiest case yet as he hunts for his friend Claude's valuable stegosaurus stamp.

❑ **Nate the Great and the Missing Key**: Nate isn't afraid to look anywhere—even under the nose of his friend's ferocious dog, Fang—to solve the case of the missing key.

❑ **Nate the Great and the Snowy Trail**: Nate has his work cut out for him when his friend Rosamond loses the birthday present she was going to give him. How can he find the present when Rosamond won't even tell him what it is?

❑ **Nate the Great and the Fishy Prize**: The trophy for the Smartest Pet Contest has disappeared! Will Sludge, Nate's clue-sniffing dog, help solve the case and prove he's worthy of the prize?

❑ **Nate the Great Stalks Stupidweed**: When his friend Oliver loses his special plant, Nate searches high and low. Who knew a little weed could be so tricky?

❑ **Nate the Great and the Boring Beach Bag**: It's no relaxing day at the beach for Nate and his trusty dog, Sludge, as they search through sand and surf for signs of a missing beach bag.

❑ **Nate the Great Goes Down in the Dumps**: Nate discovers that the only way to clean up this case is to visit the town dump. Detective work can sure get dirty!

❑ **Nate the Great and the Halloween Hunt**: It's Halloween, but Nate isn't trick-or-treating for candy. Can any of the witches, pirates, and robots he meets help him find a missing cat?

❑ **Nate the Great and the Musical Note**: Nate is used to looking for clues, not listening for them! When he gets caught in the middle of a musical riddle, can he hear his way out?

❑ **Nate the Great and the Stolen Base**: It's not easy to track down a stolen base, and Nate's hunt leads him to some strange places before he finds himself at bat once more.

❑ **Nate the Great and the Pillowcase**: When a pillowcase goes missing, Nate must venture into the dead of night to search for clues. Everyone sleeps easier knowing Nate the Great is on the case!

❑ **Nate the Great and the Mushy Valentine**: Nate hates mushy stuff. But when someone leaves a big heart taped to Sludge's doghouse, Nate must help his favorite pooch discover his secret admirer.

❑ **Nate the Great and the Tardy Tortoise**: Where did the mysterious green tortoise in Nate's yard come from? Nate needs all his patience to follow this slow . . . slow . . . clue.

❑ **Nate the Great and the Crunchy Christmas**: It's Christmas, and Fang, Annie's scary dog, is not feeling jolly. Can Nate find Fang's crunchy Christmas mail before Fang crunches on *him*?

❑ **Nate the Great Saves the King of Sweden**: Can Nate solve his *first-ever* international case without leaving his own neighborhood?

❑ **Nate the Great and Me: The Case of the Fleeing Fang**: A surprise Happy Detective Day party is great fun for Nate until his friend's dog disappears! Help Nate track down the missing pooch, and learn all the tricks of the trade in a special fun section for aspiring detectives.

❑ **Nate the Great and the Monster Mess**: Nate loves his mother's deliciously spooky Monster Cookies, but the recipe has vanished! This is one case Nate and his growling stomach can't afford to lose.

❑ **Nate the Great, San Francisco Detective**: Nate visits his cousin Olivia Sharp in the big city, but it's no vacation. Can he find a lost joke book in time to save the world?

❑ **Nate the Great and the Big Sniff**: Nate depends on his dog, Sludge, to help him solve all his cases. But Nate is on his own this time, because Sludge has disappeared! Can Nate solve the case and recover his canine buddy?

❑ **Nate the Great on the Owl Express**: Nate boards a train to guard Hoot, his cousin Olivia Sharp's pet owl. Then Hoot vanishes! Can Nate find out *whooo* took the feathered creature?